Revised edition, 1997
Text copyright ©1994, 1997 by Matthew Gollub
Illustrations copyright ©1994, 1997 by Leovigildo Martínez Torres
Printing: 3 4 5 6 7 8 9

Library of Congress Catalog Card Number: 97-90856

Publisher's Cataloging in Publication
(Prepared by Quality Books Inc.)
Gollub, Matthew.
     The moon was at a fiesta / by Matthew Gollub; pictures by
     Leovigildo Martínez. — Rev. ed.
     p. cm.
     ISBN: 1-889910-11-2 (hc)
     ISBN: 1-889910-13-9 (pb)
     SUMMARY: Jealous of the sun, the moon decides to create her own
     fiesta and celebrates a bit too much.

     1.Moon—Juvenile fiction. 2. Mexico—Juvenile fiction. I.
     Martínez, Leovigildo, ill. II. Title.

     PZ7.G583Mo 1997   [E]   QBI97-40895

To Daria and Gabrielle   M.G.

For my parents, Leovigildo and Lidia   L.M.

For hundreds of years, the sun and the moon stayed in their separate skies. It was the sun's job to shine all day long while people went about their work.

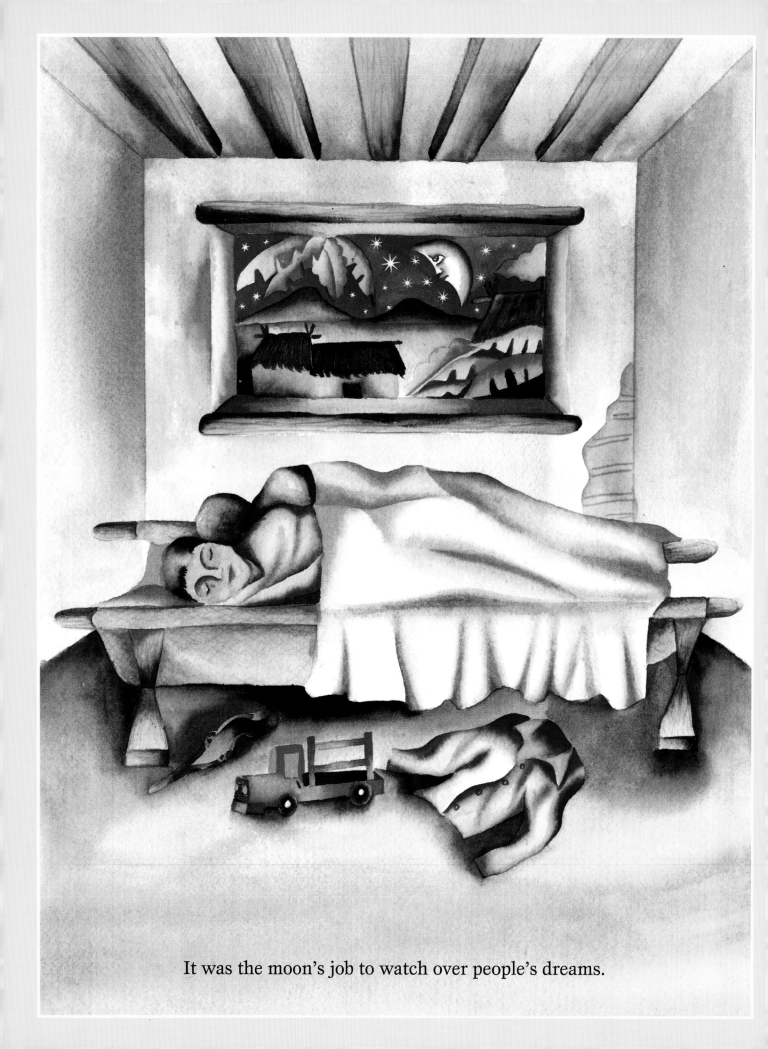

It was the moon's job to watch over people's dreams.

Both were happy with this arrangement until the night the moon overheard
the stars gossip. Some stars wished they could come out with the sun. "All the
games and feasts," they said, "take place under the sun's brilliant rays. And
those are the times when people wear their most colorful clothes."

The moon imagined how lonely she would be if the stars really left her. So she tried to learn the sun's secret for fun by staying awake while the sun was out. But sooner or later she'd nod off to sleep.

Then one afternoon, a great commotion awakened her. Bleary-eyed, she gazed down upon the earth. Fireworks mounted to toy animals spun and popped over people's heads.

Towering, stilt-legged *monigotes* were dancing round and round. The sun appeared to be enjoying himself immensely, laughing as he arched across the sky. The moon heard people call this celebration a fiesta.

It made the moon jealous to see so many people sing and parade about during the day. At night, they just slept so they could wake up early and start work in their fields. Never had she seen such merriment as this.

"I'll make my own fiesta," she decided aloud.

"You'd better not," warned the sun. "If you do, you'll fade and throw the world off balance."

Still, the moon wanted to please the restless stars, so that evening she gathered the watchmen who guarded the village at night.

"A nighttime fiesta would be magnificent!" they cried, for they too had to sleep during the day.

"Then for a fiesta," said the moon, "we'll need food and drink." She thought back on what she'd seen that afternoon. "And music," she added, "so that everyone can dance."

As other people came out of their homes to listen, the moon talked of ways to make *her* fiesta special.

"Why not have everyone bring lanterns?" clacked a *monigote*. The giant doll had stalked over, following a man who couldn't sleep.

"Lanterns at night look pretty," clattered another. This *monigote* pointed to a watchman's *farol*, and everyone agreed to bring paper lamps.

Next, the moon named *padrinos* to arrange for all the food. They hiked to a peaceful river bank where bulls, armadillos, boars, and iguanas came to drink the sweet water at night.

When the *padrinos* said they needed food for the fiesta, the animals agreed to help honor the moon.

Just then, a mermaid glided across the water. "I can bring shrimps and fish," she offered.

"Then by all means join us!" urged the hosts by the shore. The mermaid dove beneath the surface to search for tasty shellfish.

The *padrinos* decorated the site of the fiesta, and at last the awaited night arrived. The *mole*, tamales, and fish soups were ready.

People dressed in their most festive clothes and even wooden masks. Then everyone gathered amid the glow of lanterns and merrily began to eat, drink, and dance.

The moon remembered how the sun had laughed as he arched across the sky. Now, the moon felt just as pleased. She beamed on the gathering with lavish colors. The stars were so delighted they sparkled brighter than ever, and no one said a word about coming out with the sun.

The people below enjoyed themselves, too, particularly the men who offered the moon food and drink. The moon, who had never tasted food, liked the flavors so well she stayed overhead. They gave her a little more. Then a little more.

Finally, the moon ate so much food that she could no longer move across the sky. The people lost track of time, and the party went on and on. Before she knew it, the sun was rising, and the moon had forgotten to go behind the sky!

She watched the sun shine as cheerfully as ever while the people dragged themselves home to sleep. Rather than watch over people's dreams, she'd kept them out all night!

The moon, by now reduced to a glimmer, could see what trouble she had caused. Corn was not ground that morning, fields were not plowed. Crops would have to be planted late and would not grow quite as tall.

For years, the remorseful moon stayed in her evening sky as before. But she never forgot the fun that she and the stars had that night. And to this day she likes to celebrate occasionally.

That's why in Oaxaca, when people rise with the sun and see the moon, they say, "The moon was at a fiesta."